Twigs and the Wishing Pebble

Before starting any adventure, we need to do the moves that turn our magic powers on. Come on, join in.

TIME FOR TREE FU!

To make Tree Fu spells
do what you see . . .
Slide to the side,
and ***jump*** right back!
Hold your hands up high,
spin around . . .
Reach up for the sky!

Touch your nose.
Now make a ***pose***!
Clap your hands . . .
Touch your knees and
run with me.
Do what I do, to make
the ***magic***!

Look, the
sapstone in Tom's
belt is ***glowing***!
Moving turned
our magic on.

Bright and early one morning, Tom, Twigs and the Sprites were busy at Treetog's Spell School. They were learning the *Super-Grab* spell to take hold of an object and move it with magic!

“Watch this!” Twigs whispered to Tom, before adding a lickety-split, triple-stick leg-flick to his magic moves.
“Pay attention, Twigs!” Treetog called, as Twigs’ silly spell made the berries swoop around and nearly splat her!

ZOOOOOM!

Treetog decided to send Twigs on an errand, to stop him from causing more mischief.
“Please go to my library and bring back the green history book,” she asked.
“Right away!” Twigs replied, zooming off. In fact, he zoomed so fast that he crashed into one of the bookcases!

"Oof! Who put that there?"
he muttered. "It might hurt someone!"
As Twigs sat on the floor of Treetog's library, surrounded
by fallen books, he suddenly spotted something.
It was a small, shiny blue pebble!
"Wow! What's this?" Twigs wondered. He quickly 
grabbed it, along with the green book.

A little later, the lesson was finished and it was time for lunch. Twigs and Tom sat down with a Trillicake each.
"Mmm. I love Trillicakes!" Tom mumbled through a mouthful.
"Me too!" Twigs agreed, taking another bite. "I wish they were a bit bigger though."

Just then, both Tom and Twigs' Trillicakes began to glow with a bright blue light . . . And then they got bigger!
"What just happened?" Tom gasped, holding up his new, larger Trillicake.

Twigs saw that his new pebble was
glowing blue.
"It's a **MAGIC WISHING PEBBLE**!"
he cried, jumping up excitedly.
"Imagine all the fun we can have
with this . . . Let's go and show
the others!"

"It doesn't belong to you, Twigs. You should take it back to Treelog straight away," Ariela said, when Twigs told his friends about the magic pebble.

"Okay, okay," Twigs sighed, knowing that she was right.

The friends hadn't noticed that the Mushas, Stink and Puffy, were nearby and had heard every word.

"We need to get our hands on that wishing pebble!" cried Puffy.

"Yeah! Imagine all the mischief we could make!" chuckled Stink.

"I'll go now, right away. The magic pebble will be back in Treetog's library quick as a flash!" Twigs declared as he raced away. But he was racing so fast that he tripped! The pebble flew out of his hand . . .

BOUNCE!

BOUNCE!

BOUNCE!

. . . and into the hands of Puffy and Stink! They couldn't believe their luck!

"Oh no! We've got to do something!" Twigs cried, as the Mushas ran away with the pebble.

As they ran, Puffy and Stink quickly came up with a plan. They would use their wishes to make a big mess in Treetopolis!

OOOOH!

"I wish for the streets to be covered in lots and lots of slime!"
Puffy said, grinning.
"I wish for the streets to be covered in *more* slime!" replied
Stink, snatching the pebble.
Puffy snatched it back and wished for **EVEN MORE SLIME!**

As the Mushas wished back and forth, the pebble glowed bright blue and slime started to flow down the streets of Treetopolis. A wave of thick green slime rose over the buildings, covering the windows and the doors. Puffy and Stink laughed and clapped at the mess they'd made!

BRRRR!

Tom and Twigs had to stop the slime, before it covered Treetopolis. But how could they get the wishing pebble from the Mushas?

"*Easy-Freezy*!" Twigs called, quickly casting a spell that froze the Mushas in a block of ice. It worked! Tom grabbed the wishing pebble, as the slime flowed closer and closer.

"We're going to need **BIG WORLD MAGIC** to suck all of the Mushas' wishes back into the wishing pebble. We've got to make the slime disappear before it covers Treetopolis! So I need your help. It's time to do the *Magic-Go-Back* spell. Are you ready?"

TREE FU GO!

"Into your spell pose."

"Start with your palms together, fingers crossed."

"Kick one leg back. Kick your other leg back."

"Shake low on one side. Shake low on the other side."

"Shake it high on one side. Shake it high on the other side."

"Zoom your hands up the centre, and un-do them!"

"Now clap and say 'Magic-Go-Back' to send the magic to me. 'Magic-Go-Back!'"

"Look, the magic is working!"

Slowly, the pebble rose up into the air and began to shudder and shake, before suddenly bursting into lots of little pieces in a flash of light – sucking the Mushas' slime wishes back! Magically, the slime started to retreat, moving back through the streets until it had all disappeared.

MAGIC-GO-BACK!

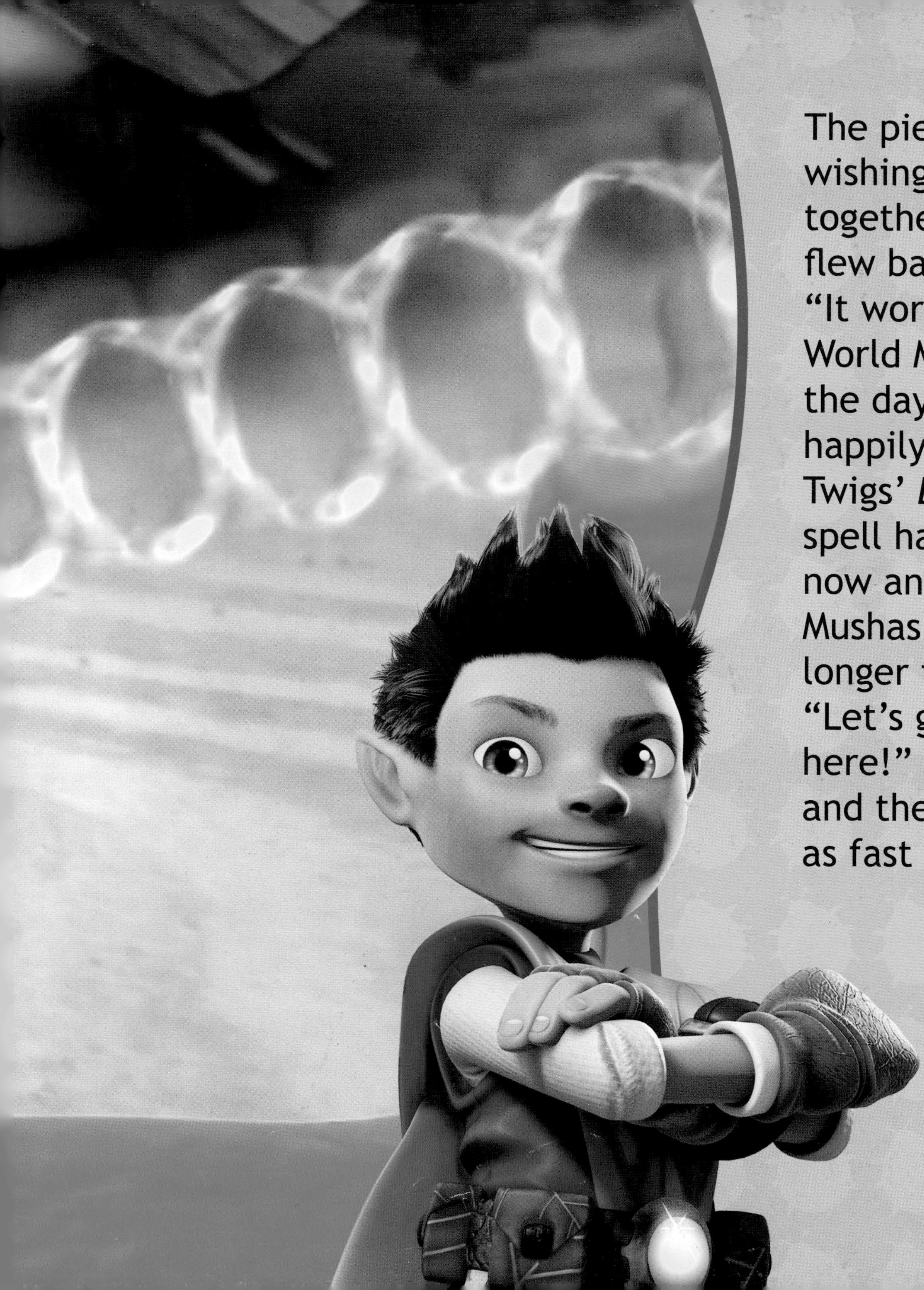

The pieces of the wishing pebble came together again and flew back to Tom.
"It worked. Big World Magic saved the day!" he laughed happily.
Twigs' *Easy-Freezy* spell had worn off now and so the Mushas were no longer frozen.
"Let's get out of here!" Puffy cried, and they ran away as fast as they could.

"Sorry for causing all this trouble, Tom," Twigs said. He felt really bad about taking the wishing pebble. "You might have caused some problems, but your last spell helped solve a few problems, too!" Tom replied, grinning at his friend. "Now, let's get that pebble back to Treetog before anything else goes wrong!"

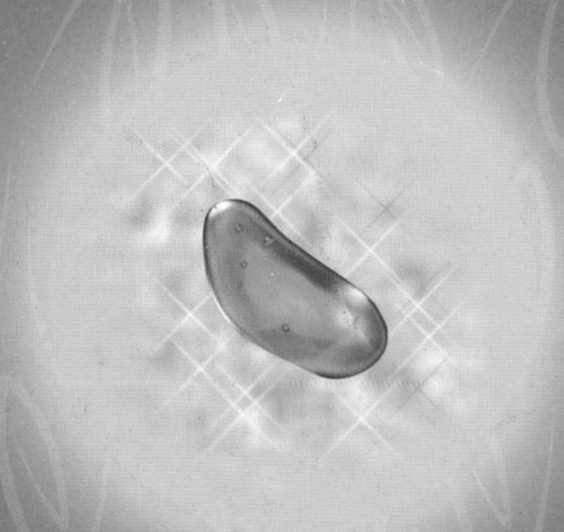

The Random House Group Limited supports the Forest Stewardship Council® (FSC®), the leading international forest certification organization. Our books carrying the FSC label are printed on FSC®-certified paper. FSC is the only forest certification scheme endorsed by the leading environmental organizations, including Greenpeace. Our paper procurement policy can be found at www.randomhouse.co.uk/environment